CW00973042

THE MILKY WAY KIDS

AND THE SPACE SCHOOL ROBOT

Written by
Camilla & Freddy
Vinterstø Halstensen

For our beloved Theodor.
May you always have the strength and freedom to follow your
heart and to be the truest version of yourself.

And Mats and Udesh, thank you.
You have our eternal gratitude.

Published in association with
Bear With Us Productions

© 2022 Camilla & Freddy
Vinterstø Halstensen
The Milky Way Kids

The right of Camilla Vinterstø Halstensen
and Freddy Vinterstø Halstensen as the
authors of this work has been asserted
by them in accordance with the Copyright
Designs and Patents Act 1988.
All rights reserved, including the right of
reproduction in whole or part in any form.

ISBN: Hardcover 978-82-693063-0-9
         Paperback 978-82-693063-2-3

Cover by Richie Evans
Design by Tommaso Pigliapochi
Illustrated by Jenny Yevheniia Lisovaya

www.justbearwithus.com

Illustrated by
Jenny Yevheniia Lisovaya

THE MILKY WAY KIDS
AND THE SPACE SCHOOL ROBOT

Written by
**Camilla & Freddy
Vinterstø Halstensen**

This book belongs to:

....

....

In the Milky Way, there are many planets yet to be discovered. Some of these planets are home to very special people, who are quite similar to humans. The big difference is that they have brightly colored bodies.

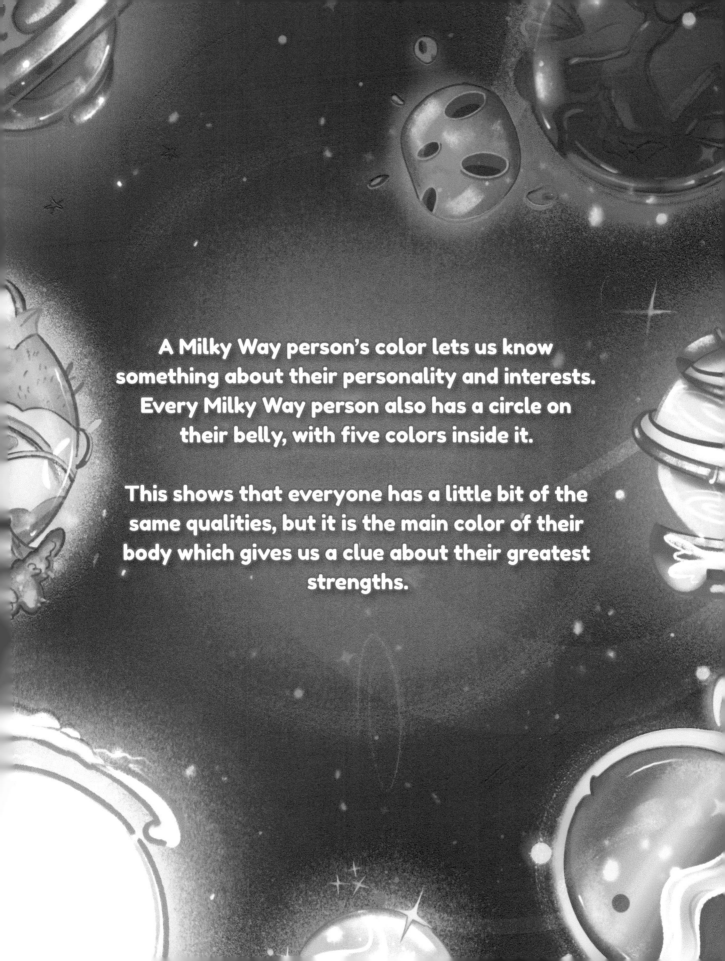

A Milky Way person's color lets us know something about their personality and interests. Every Milky Way person also has a circle on their belly, with five colors inside it.

This shows that everyone has a little bit of the same qualities, but it is the main color of their body which gives us a clue about their greatest strengths.

Blue people enjoy sports and being outdoors. They also have a technical mind. This means they understand how things work and like to fix them when they're broken.

Purple people are creative and have big imaginations. Often they are introverted, which means they can seem a little bit shy. They're also good at knowing how other people are feeling.

Yellow people are extroverted, which means they appear very confident. They're usually energetic and good at being the leader.

Green people enjoy science, reading and research. They have a mathematical mind, which means they're very good with numbers and making calculations.

Red people are passionate. This means they're really keen to help others. They are loving toward animals and really loyal to their friends.

Just before you start the story,

which do you think

might be your

MAIN COLORS?

Across the galaxy, it was the start of a
new space school year.

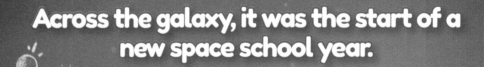

Little Doret was dropped off on the planet Scolar, where
kids of the Milky Way went to school.
She waved goodbye to her moms, who flew away in their
bubble ship. Since it was the first day back, Doret was
feeling shyer than normal.

She didn't speak to any of the children in the schoolyard.
Instead, Doret began to daydream.

Playing by herself, Doret dreamed she was diving into the ocean. In her head, she imagined she was still swimming on the planet of Pytti.

Her moms had taken her to the watery world for a great vacation. There were so many beautiful creatures to play with in the ocean.

Suddenly, Doret stopped swimming. She saw a very strange creature that didn't belong beneath the waves.

Doret's daydream disappeared. She realized that the strange creature was actually standing in the schoolyard! The creature wasn't colorful at all. It was completely black and shiny, as if it was made of metal. Could it be a robot? Doret felt a little bit nervous.

"Hello" she said in a small voice, "Can you speak?" The creature didn't reply. Instead, it turned its head toward one of its back legs. Doret crept closer. She could see the leg was cracked.

Doret thought for a moment. Fixing things wasn't one of her best strengths. She preferred being creative. Doret decided to sneak the limping robot inside. Maybe one of her classmates would be able to help.

Doret was quite shy and liked doing things by herself, such as drawing or listening to music.
As she crossed the yard, the students were surprised.
They didn't expect her to have a robot friend.

On the other side of the yard, sporty Golis raced across the Astroturf. He was the best hypersprinter in the whole space school.

Students competing in the hypersprint wore special rocket boots, which made them run really fast. As Golis crossed the finishing line, one of his boots spluttered, stuttered... and completely stopped!

He tumbled to the ground and landed really hard on his bottom. Golis looked around and saw the big dent he had made in the Astroturf.

"At least I won the race" He beamed proudly.

Golis lived with his dad and the two of them
spent a lot of time together. When they weren't
camping in the jungles of Vegari, they'd be fixing
Dad's bubble ship in the space dock.
Golis had a pretty good idea how to mend his broken rocket boot.
He picked it off the ground and headed into
the school's laboratory.

Golis was shocked to see Doret in the laboratory. The two children usually had very different hobbies.

He was even more surprised to see Doret's metal companion waiting on a workbench.

"I think it's a robot," said Doret shyly, "and it's got a broken leg. Can you help?"
"You're right'." Golis nodded.
"This robot also has rocket feet. That's awesome!"
Very quickly, Golis found the right tool and repaired the robot's cracked leg.

Suddenly, Doret heard a noise outside the room.
"Someone's coming!" she whispered.

Faster than he'd ever moved before
(even in rocket boots), Golis hid the robot
under the workbench.
Principal Flux came into the laboratory and
frowned at the two students.

"What's going on here?" he asked.
"Nothing," replied Golis. "We're just working on my
technology assignment."
"Very well," said Principal Flux as he left the room.
"That was close," said Doret. "Now, we need to find out
what kind of robot this is."

Golis smiled.
"I know someone who might be able to help with that!"

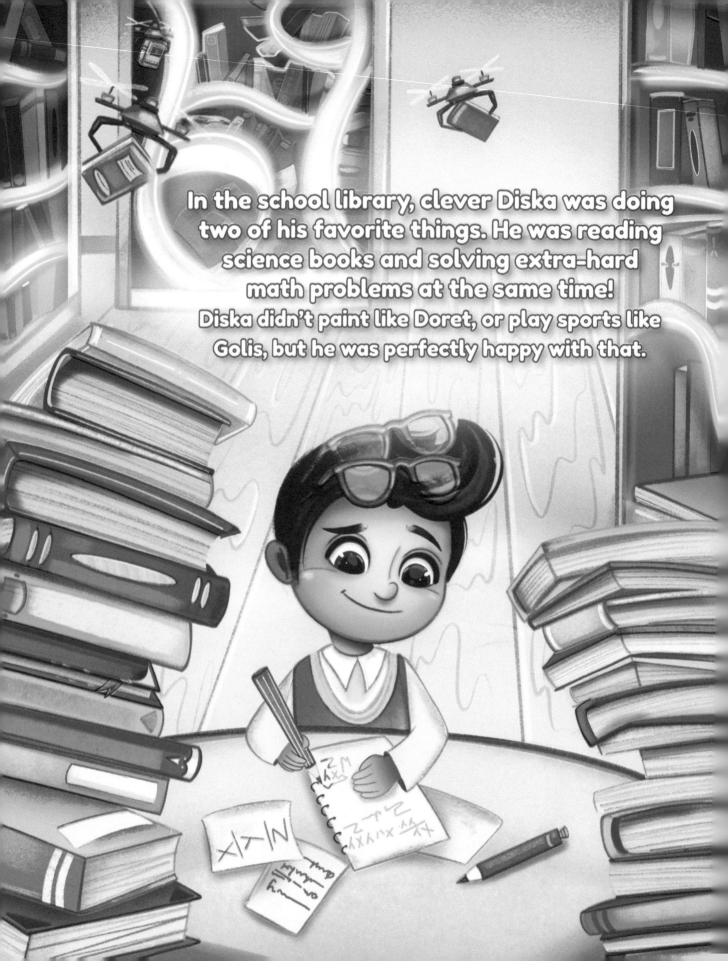

In the school library, clever Diska was doing two of his favorite things. He was reading science books and solving extra-hard math problems at the same time! Diska didn't paint like Doret, or play sports like Golis, but he was perfectly happy with that.

Diska looked up in surprise when Doret and Golis arrived in the library. "You've found a robot!" he said with excitement.

Diska jumped onto the table. "I was reading about robots just the other day. Now where did I put that book?" He grabbed an old textbook from the tower beside him and blew all the dust off its cover.

"Achoo!"
Doret and Golis sneezed.

As he turned the pages of the textbook, Diska's green face became paler. "What's wrong?" asked Golis. "Why do you look so worried?"

Diska turned the textbook around. On the pages were pictures of creatures that looked like Doret's robot. "My research could be wrong," said Diska, "but I think this robot is a Monozoid. A robot from the planet Darko!"

Doret and Golis **screamed.** Darko was the scariest place in the galaxy. A forbidden planet no one had ever been to, but every Milky Way kid knew what lived there... color-eating monsters!

"Aaaaah!"

shouted Diska, who didn't want to miss out on the screaming. Hearing the high-pitched sound, the Monozoid backed away.

Suddenly, it grew as tall as the ceiling and bashed into the bookcase. Hundreds of books tumbled to the floor.

The library door opened with a

sWOOSh

Diska, who'd researched robots, pointed to a switch on the creature's leg.

Sporty Golis leaped and quickly flicked the switch... making the Monozoid turn invisible! He was just in time.

Principal Flux was back again.
"What's going on in here?" Principal Flux frowned.
"We're rearranging the library," said Diska, surrounded by a mountain of books.
"Very well," said Principal Flux as he left the library.

Once the principal had gone, Diska turned off the robot's invisibility.

"Why did the Monozoid grow so tall?" asked Golis.
"Is it trying to scare us?" Doret thought for a moment.
"Maybe Monozoids grow bigger when they feel scared,"
she said.
"I understand if it feels frightened or alone.
The robot is a long way from its home planet."
Before anyone could reply, the library door opened again.
"Who was screaming?" asked Niramit.
"Did I miss all the fun?"

Niramit loved making a dramatic entrance. Confident and loud, she liked performing and taking charge of most situations. When Niramit saw the Monozoid, her eyes opened wide. She crossed the library floor with big strides.
"A robot!" she shouted. 'That's so cool!"
"Be careful," warned Diska.
"It's from the planet Darko."
But Niramit wasn't scared of the robot at all.

"Want to hear a joke?" Niramit asked the metal creature. "Why did the robot fail his school exam? Because... he was a little rusty!" Niramit snickered and the other kids joined in. To their surprise, the Monozoid started shaking with a

whirr whirr whirr

The robot was laughing!

woof WOOF woof!

There was another new noise in the room.

The Milky Way Kids looked around the room.
Orion the galactic retriever poked its head
through a pile of books.

The puppy's owner wasn't far behind.
"There you are, Orion," said Gosago.
This caring child loved all space animals,
but Orion most of all.
He even persuaded Principal Flux that the cheeky puppy
could come to school. Orion leaped across the library
and began licking the metal Monozoid.
Suddenly, the robot shrank to its normal size.

The puppy and the robot chased each other across the library. They were having great fun running rings around the room.

"That mended metal leg looks as good as new," Golis commented with an approving nod.
"I don't think the Monozoid is scared anymore," said Doret. "It just wanted some company. After all, it must miss its family."
"That's awful," said Gosago.
"We've got to help it. What can we do?"
"I have a plan!" said Niramit.
"Everyone... follow me."

The Milky Way Kids snuck along the space school's corridor. They didn't want to get caught, even though the Monozoid was invisible.

"The school has its own bubble ship," whispered Niramit, who was leading the way. "It's used for school trips, but we can use it to take the robot home to Darko."

Doret was feeling nervous, but also a little bit excited. This was the kind of adventure she daydreamed about. It was really nice to be going on one with friends.

"How will we fly the spaceship?" she asked.

"Leave that to me," said technical Golis.

"Dad and I go flying together all the time."

Quietly, the five friends crept into the school's dark space dock, followed by Orion and the robot.

Flash!

The lights turned on.
It was a trap!

Today's Cosmic Weather Forecast

Principal Flux was waiting in front of the spaceship.
He wasn't surprised to see the children, or
even their shiny black robot.
"I know what's going on" he said with a frown.
"You're planning to borrow this bubble ship.
Space school principals have eyes everywhere."
"Please don't stop us," pleaded Gosago.
"This robot isn't colorful like us, but that doesn't make it scary.
It's just different. You have to let us help this creature."

Principal Flux's frown disappeared. Gosago's passionate speech had changed his mind.

"I'm not going to stop you," he said, pressing a button on the bubble ship. The side of the spacecraft opened and the engines burst to life. "You've gotten this far by using all of your skills together" Principal Flux smiled. "You've helped a lost, broken robot and now it's time to take it home. Fly carefully!"

SCHOLAR SPACE SCHOOL

The Monozoid, the puppy and the Milky Way
Kids crammed into the cockpit.
Once everyone was buckled in, clever Diska
opened his math notebook.

"I've made some calculations," he said, "and worked out
a route that takes us to Darko."
"Great work," said Niramit, sitting in the central chair.
"Golis, please fly us out of here"
The bubble ship blasted off and out of
Scolar's atmosphere.

Soon, the super-fast spacecraft was in orbit, high above Darko. From here, it was hard to see anything on the black planet.

The Monozoid bounced eagerly when it saw its home world below. It was time for the kids to say goodbye to their metal friend.
Caring Gosago had tears in his eyes.
"Please don't break any more legs," he said.
"I hope we'll see you again," whispered Doret.
"We don't know much about your world."

The children and Orion watched through the ship's window as the Monozoid stepped out of the air lock and floated into space. The robot took one last look at its new friends, then blasted down to the planet.

Flames roa**red** from its rocket feet.

"I'd love rocket feet like that," sighed Golis.
"I might win the hypersprint at the next Galactic Games!"
Niramit beamed a huge smile. "Well done everyone,"
she said, "Our mission is complete!"
"The robot will be reunited with its family."
"Let's fly this bubble ship back to school."
Niramit was right. It was time for the Milky Way Kids to
return to school and see their own families again.

Doret's moms were delighted to hear about their daughter's fantastic adventure. They were also pleased that she had made some friends at school. Just before bedtime, Doret drew several pictures, remembering all that had happened since she met the Monozoid. She smiled when she realized that her and her new friends made up all the five colors of the circle.

As Doret drifted off to sleep, she began to dream. In her incredible imagination, the Milky Way Kids were flying through the galaxy in their bubble ship.

Which strange new planets would they discover next? Doret knew one thing was certain: when her friends worked as a team, there wasn't any problem they couldn't solve together.

Ingram Content Group UK Ltd.
Milton Keynes UK
UKHW050933130623
423339UK00002B/12